The ^{Very} Fairy Princess

Here Comes the Flower Girl!

by Julie Andrews & Emma Walton Hamilton

Illustrated by

Christine Davenier

Little, Brown and Company

New York   Boston

Hi! I'm Geraldine.
I'm a fairy princess.
Hardly anyone believes me,
but I have a sparkly feeling inside
that tells me it's TRUE.

I spend most of my time spreading my sparkle however I can.
For instance, I always conduct myself in a princess-ly fashion.
(My wings and crown help, of course.)

I add a creative touch to everything I do,
and I try to make someone smile at least once a day.
(Fairy princesses care a LOT about the happiness of their people.)

Today I got
some FANTASTIC news!
My aunt Sue is getting married
to Mr. Flanigan, the fire chief. And guess what?
I get to be their flower girl! PERFECT!
I can just picture myself walking down the aisle with Aunt Sue
in her long white wedding dress, with the organ music playing
and HUNDREDS of people smiling all around us!

Mom says that's not EXACTLY
the way it's going to be.
Aunt Sue wants to get married
right here … in our garden!

At first I'm disappointed, but then I realize that means
I can put my royal stamp on EVERYTHING
and make sure there's PLENTY of sparkle.
(Fairy princesses are at their best on festive occasions.)

We don't have much time, so we have to get to work RIGHT away.

Daddy mows the lawn, and Mommy prunes the roses.

My brother, Stewart, practices "Here Comes the Bride" on his trumpet.

It's MY job to make everything look as SPARKLY as possible.

I hang ribbons on the bushes and stick hearts in the flowerbeds.

I start to paint HUGE glittery signs, but Mom says sometimes less is more.

So I paint smaller signs,
using my BRIGHTEST colors
and just a dash of pink glitter.
(Fairy princesses know how
to make a little go a long way.)

Time to make the wedding cake!
I suggest three layers—
one chocolate,
one banana,
and one red velvet—
with raspberry filling,
a marzipan shell,
and vanilla icing.

Dad says Aunt Sue prefers a simple lemon cake, but I can help decorate it.
I use as many bells, sprinkles, and flowers as I can!
(Fairy princesses have exquisite taste.)

I start to fill little bags with rice to throw at the bride and groom,
but Stewart tells me rice isn't used anymore because it's bad for the birds.
It makes them explode.

YIKES!
We use birdseed instead.
(Any fairy princess knows that exploding
birds can RUIN a wedding.)

I have to practice my flower-girl walk.

Petal-tossing can be tricky,
and I need to get it just right!

I discover that the petals go higher if I add some pirouettes and leaps, but Mom says a simple step-together princess walk is best for a wedding.

(Even a fairy princess has to learn the art of compromise.)

Finally, the big day arrives.

I leap out of bed and throw open the curtains. It's RAINING!

All my decorations are a soggy mess. What a DISASTER!

This is going to be the most UN-sparkly day in wedding history!

Aunt Sue arrives with Grandma.

"Rain on a wedding is good luck," Grandma says.

I'm not sure Aunt Sue agrees.

We go up to my bedroom to get dressed.
Aunt Sue hands me a big box.
It's my flower-girl dress!
I hope it's made of silk, covered with
flowers, and has LOTS of petticoats.

It turns out to be plain white cotton
with holes in it. Aunt Sue explains that it's the same
material as her dress, and it's called "eyelet."
I think it's more of an "eyesore."
Aunt Sue looks at me.
"Hmm. Something's MISSING...."

"I know! My very fairy
flower-girl princess needs her
wings and crown!" HOORAY!
I dash for the closet
and pull out my favorite
wings and tiara.
Aunt Sue nods. "Perfect!"
She even lets me wear
my pink high-tops.

Now I feel my sparkle returning!
And I have to admit,
Aunt Sue looks pretty in her dress, too.
The wedding is about to begin!

We rush downstairs and find a surprise — the rain has stopped!
Everyone is waiting for us in the garden. I get to go first,
in front of Aunt Sue. My heart is pounding with excitement!

Stewart plays his trumpet, and everyone stands up.

I do my BEST princess walk, scattering

my rose petals in graceful arcs.

(Very fairy princesses always shine when they're in the spotlight!)

The minister says
the marrying words,
and Aunt Sue and Mr. Flanigan say "I do."
Mr. Flanigan slips the ring
on Aunt Sue's finger, and they kiss.
Aunt Sue's eyes SPARKLE
with love and happiness. Daddy hugs Mommy.
Grandma wipes a tear from her cheek, and EVERYONE cheers.

I suddenly realize that the RIGHT kind of sparkle
is all it takes to make a PERFECT day!

For Liza, whose brilliant SPARKLE *makes our*
Gerry's all the brighter.
—J.A. & E.W.H.

Pour Henriette Bouland ma grand-mère qui vient de nous quitter avant
de fêter ses 104 printemps. Tous les souvenirs d'enfance qu'elle m'a si précieusement
aidé à construire continueront à m'inspirer. You fill my life with SPARKLE!
—C.D.

The illustrations for this book were done in ink and color pencil on Kaecolor paper. · *The text was set in Baskerville, and the display type is Mayfair.*

Copyright © 2012 by Julie Andrews Trust—1989 and Beech Tree Books, LLC · Illustrations copyright © 2012 by Christine Davenier · All rights reserved. Except as permitted under the U.S. Copyright Act of 1976, no part of this publication may be reproduced, distributed, or transmitted in any form or by any means, or stored in a database or retrieval system, without the prior written permission of the publisher. · Little, Brown and Company · Hachette Book Group · 237 Park Avenue, New York, NY 10017 · Visit our website at www.lb-kids.com · Little, Brown and Company is a division of Hachette Book Group, Inc. · The Little, Brown name and logo are trademarks of Hachette Book Group, Inc. · The publisher is not responsible for websites (or their content) that are not owned by the publisher. · First edition: April 2012 · Library of Congress Cataloging-in-Publication Data · Andrews, Julie. · The very fairy princess: Here comes the flower girl! / by Julie Andrews and Emma Walton Hamilton ; illustrated by Christine Davenier. — 1st ed. · p. cm. · Summary: When disaster strikes in the form of rain on Aunt Sue's wedding day, flower girl and self-proclaimed fairy princess Geraldine finds a way to bring sunshine to the party, reminding everyone that the most important thing at a wedding is the most special sparkle of all—happiness and love. · ISBN 978-0-316-18561-5 · [1. Flower girls—Fiction. 2. Weddings—Fiction. 3. Princesses—Fiction.] · I. Hamilton, Emma Walton. · II. Davenier, Christine, ill. · III. Title. · PZ7.A5673Vg 2012 [E]—dc23 · 2011026375 · 10 9 8 7 6 5 4 3 2 1 · IM · Printed in China